This book belongs to

....

Illustrated by Pamela Storey
Original story by Geoffrey Alan
Adapted by Lynne Gibbs

Published in Great Britain by Brimax Publishing Ltd
Appledram Barns, Chichester PO20 7EQ

Published in the US by Byeway Books Inc,
Lenexa KS 66219 Tel 866.4BYEWAY
www.byewaybooks.com

© Brimax Publishing Ltd 2005

Printed in China

Bramble Bear

The missing necklace

BRIMAX

On his way up to bed one night, Bramble Bear noticed that his dad was reading a detective book.

"Dad, what does a detective do?" asked Bramble.

"He hunts for clues and solves mysteries," said Bramble's dad.

"Wow! That sounds exciting. But is it very hard?" asked Bramble.

"Not always," smiled Dad, as Bramble climbed on to his lap. "I mean, I know you've been in the cookie jar!"

"You do?" gasped Bramble, looking surprised. "But how do you know?"

"Because you have crumbs on your chin!" laughed Bramble's dad.

"I wish I were a detective," yawned Bramble, closing his eyes.

Next morning, Bramble borrowed his dad's magnifying glass. Then off he went, pretending to be a detective!

As he walked along a path, Bramble stopped to take a closer look at a spider, dangling from a leaf.

"It's HUGE!" gulped Bramble, who had forgotten how big a magnifying glass makes things seem.

"I wonder who made those?" said Bramble when he saw some BIG prints in the ground. "It's a mystery – and I'm just the bear to solve it!"

Bramble followed the tracks to a river. They led straight into the water!

"Perhaps it's a monster frog!" said Bramble. "I must find out. That's what a real detective would do."

Bramble tiptoed on to an old wooden bridge and peered over the side.

"If it is a monster frog in the water, I'll soon see it," said Bramble.

Suddenly, the little bear detective saw bubbles rising to the surface of the water. Then he heard a strange noise!

"Ooh, a monster frog that makes glug, glug, glug noises!" gasped Bramble.

Then, just as Bramble saw something sparkling in the sunlight, a dark figure sprang from the water!

"Hello, there!" called Bramble's dad.

"Oh, h-hello," said Bramble. "I thought you were a monster frog!"

"Hardly!" laughed Bramble's dad. "Your mother lost her necklace here and I have been searching for it."

When Bramble saw the big flippers that his dad was wearing he laughed, "So a monster frog didn't make those prints in the ground!"

"No, it was my flippers!" laughed Bramble's dad.

"I saw something sparkling in the sunlight," said Bramble, excitedly. "I wonder if I can find it again?"

"Here it is," said Bramble. "The necklace didn't fall in the water. It was hooked on to the bottom of the bridge!"

"Well done," said Bramble's dad. "However did you know?"

"Oh, clues, I suppose... or it may just have been good luck," said Bramble.

"Good detective work, you mean," said Bramble's dad.

Back home, Bramble gave his mother her lost necklace – and she gave him a big, big hug!

"I hope you didn't mind me using your magnifying glass, Dad?" said Bramble.

"You can keep it," said Bramble's dad. "A good detective always needs a magnifying glass!"

Bramble looked a little embarrassed.

"Thank you," said Bramble, "but I don't think I want to be a detective anymore."

"Why not?" asked Bramble's dad.

"Well," began Bramble, "if I had seen a real monster frog, I would have been very frightened!"

"Oh, Bramble," smiled Dad, putting his arm around his son's shoulders, "you are a funny little bear."

What can you see?

Can you point to these pictures as you find them in the story?

magnifying glass

spider

book

flippers

necklace

frog